MARY ENGELBREIT'S

Little Book of Love

HARPER

An Imprint of HarperCollinsPublishers

Mary Engelbreit's Little Book of Love
Copyright © 2020 by Mary Engelbreit Enterprises, Inc.
All rights reserved. Manufactured in Italy.

www.harpercollinschildrens.com
Library of Congress Control Number: 2020937200
ISBN 978-0-06-301722-1

20 21 22 23 24   RTLO   10 9 8 7 6 5 4 3 2 1
❖
First Edition

For my love, Phil

"If you have only one
smile in you, give it to
the people you love."

—Maya Angelou

"There is no charm equal
to tenderness of heart."

—Jane Austen

"Let thyself be taught
to love by rule and
hate by measure."

—Johann Wolfgang Von Goethe

"All, everything that I understand, I understand only because I love."

—Leo Tolstoy

"The best and most beautiful things in the world cannot be seen nor even touched, but just felt in the heart."

—Helen Keller

"*Life without love*
is like a tree without
blossom and fruit."

—Kahlil Gibran

"i carry your heart
(i carry it in my heart)"

—e. e. cummings

"Till I loved I never lived."

—Emily Dickinson

"Life is a flower of
which love is the honey."

—Victor Hugo

"Love takes off the masks that we fear we cannot live without."

—James Baldwin

"Friendship is the only
cement that will ever hold
the world together."

—Woodrow Wilson

"Love is something more splendid than mere kindness."

—C. S. Lewis

"There is no remedy for love but to love more."

—Henry David Thoreau

"Love is a better teacher
than a sense of duty."

—Albert Einstein

"It is my firm belief that it is love that sustains the earth. There only is life where there is love."

—Mahatma Gandhi

"I still believe that
love is the most durable
power in the world."

—Martin Luther King Jr.

"Love is a fruit in season
at all times and within
reach of every hand."

—Mother Teresa

"Love, I find,
is like singing."

—Zora Neale Hurston

"To me, you will
be unique in all the world.
To you, I shall be unique
in all the world."

—Antoine de Saint-Exupéry

"To love oneself
is the beginning of
a lifelong romance."

—Oscar Wilde

"Love loves
to love love."

—James Joyce

"This is what I know for sure:
Love is all around."

—Oprah Winfrey

"Love all, trust a few,
do wrong to none."

—William Shakespeare

"If a thing loves,
it is infinite."

—William Blake